the VERY WORST ever

NOT ReaDy PlaYeR One

BY ANDY NONAMUS
ILLUSTRATED BY AMY JINDRA

LITTLE SIMON
NEW YORK   AMSTERDAM/ANTWERP   LONDON
TORONTO   SYDNEY/MELBOURNE   NEW DELHI

This book is a work of fiction. Any references to historical events, real people, or real places are used fictitiously. Other names, characters, places, and events are products of the author's imagination, and any resemblance to actual events or places or persons, living or dead, is entirely coincidental.

LITTLE SIMON
An imprint of Simon & Schuster Children's Publishing Division
1230 Avenue of the Americas, New York, New York 10020
First Little Simon hardcover edition September 2025
© 2025 by Simon & Schuster, LLC
Also available in a Little Simon paperback edition.
All rights reserved, including the right of reproduction in whole or in part in any form.
LITTLE SIMON is a registered trademark of Simon & Schuster, LLC, and associated colophon is a trademark of Simon & Schuster, LLC.
For information about special discounts for bulk purchases, please contact Simon & Schuster Special Sales at 1-866-506-1949 or business@simonandschuster.com.
The Simon & Schuster Speakers Bureau can bring authors to your live event. For more information or to book an event, contact the Simon & Schuster Speakers Bureau at 1-866-248-3049 or visit our website at www.simonspeakers.com.
Text by Matthew J. Gilbert
Book design by Hannah Frece
The illustrations for this book were rendered digitally.
The text of this book was set in Causten Round.
Manufactured in the United States of America 0825 LAK
10 9 8 7 6 5 4 3 2 1
Library of Congress Cataloging-in-Publication Data
Names: Nonamus, Andy author | Jindra, Amy illustrator
Title: Not ready player one / by Andy Nonamus ; illustrated by Amy Jindra.
Description: New York : Little Simon, 2025. | Series: The very worst ever ; book 9 | Audience term: Children | Summary: A very unlucky kid who is notoriously bad at video games agrees to help a friend with her new virtual reality game, Perfect Pixel Pups.
Identifiers: LCCN 2025006669 (print) | LCCN 2025006670 (ebook) | ISBN 9781665973564 paperback | ISBN 9781665973571 hardcover | ISBN 9781665973588 ebook
Subjects: LCSH: Friendship—Fiction | CYAC: Video games—Fiction | Virtual reality—Fiction | LCGFT: Fiction
Classification: LCC PZ7.1.N6378 No 2025 (print) | LCC PZ7.1.N6378 (ebook) | DDC [Fic]—dc23/eng/20250520
LC record available at https://lccn.loc.gov/2025006669
LC ebook record available at https://lccn.loc.gov/2025006670

CONTENTS

INTRODUCTION LETTER

CHAPTER 1	*EXTRA* EXTRA CREDIT	1
CHAPTER 2	INTRUDER! INTRUDER!	13
CHAPTER 3	CHEAT CODE UNLOCKED	31
CHAPTER 4	THE MINI BOSS GAME	45
CHAPTER 5	NOT READY, PLAYER ONE!	59
CHAPTER 6	THE GAME STRIKES BACK!	73
CHAPTER 7	DON'T HOLD YOUR BREATH	85
CHAPTER 8	PLAYER TWO GOES BOOM!	93
CHAPTER 9	AS EASY AS PIE	103
CHAPTER 10	GAME OVER	113

Hey, Reader!

Thanks for checking out my story. Though I gotta warn you, I can't ever let you know my real name or what I look like. This may seem weird, but trust me, it's very important that I stay a secret.

Why? To protect myself! Seriously, these stories are super embarrassing!

Plus, you might even know me already! I could be in your class, or in the cactus gardening club, in the underwater soccer club, or stuck on the playground monkey bars during recess . . . anywhere!

Hi!

For all you know I could be sitting next to you right now!

So I went ahead and scratched out my name and put a sticker on my face, so you don't have to. You're welcome.

Now, we can both enjoy reading all about my awkward life . . . if you're into that kind of thing.

Peace out!
▬▬▬▬▬▬

# 1

EXTRA EXTRA CREDIT

Ah, video games. We have a not-so-great history together. Don't get me wrong, I love video games.

Where else can you race a car upside down? Or save kittens from a spooky castle? Or find a buried treasure of lost kittens inside a spooky castle while driving upside down?

So yeah, I play video games.

I'm just not the best at them. It's more like I find new and exciting ways to lose.

There was the time I fell into a pit before the game even started and the screen froze for three hours.

Or the time my mom learned cheat codes and kept destroying me over and over and over again. Yep, I can't even win against my mom!

Another time I was playing a game on Mom's phone and I thought I was winning, but I was actually ordering twenty pizzas and a robot octopus (or Robo-Octo) from an online store.

We kept the pizzas, but Robo-Octo ran away. Hmm, I wonder where he went?

So why am I telling you this? Because you need to understand why I can't help my friend, Regina du Lar, with her extra-credit project for class.

I am NOT a gamer.

There we were, in the back of Regina's family limo.

"You gotta help me! Puhhhleeease!!!" Regina said. "It's just a game!"

"You know me and games," I reminded her. "I'm the worst kid possible for this."

"No! That's why you are PERFECT!" said Regina. "My game is for people who are really bad at video games. And you are *really, really* bad."

Hmm, I wasn't sure how to feel about that.

"Thanks, I think," I said.

Regina smiled and asked, "So, you'll do it? Can I count on you?"

Sometimes in life you get stuck between two problems. I didn't want to embarrass myself yet again. But I also didn't want to let my friend down.

What else could I say but, "Hey, you can *always* count on me to be the worst."

2

INTRUDER! INTRUDER!

The limo didn't take us to Regina's house. Instead, we zoomed through a secret tunnel underneath the city. I felt like a superhero racing to my secret lair.

This was all very normal for Regina because Regina wasn't like other kids.

For starters, she designed video games for fun.

Also, she was the only classmate I knew who had an office *in a SKYSCRAPER*!

When we reached the building, I thought the limo would park outside. Instead, we drove into a giant elevator that lifted the limo higher and higher.

"You've arrived at the top floor of Du Lar Video Game Headquarters," the driver announced.

"C'mon," Regina said. "My game's waiting."

I followed Regina to a door where a red light scanned us head to toe.

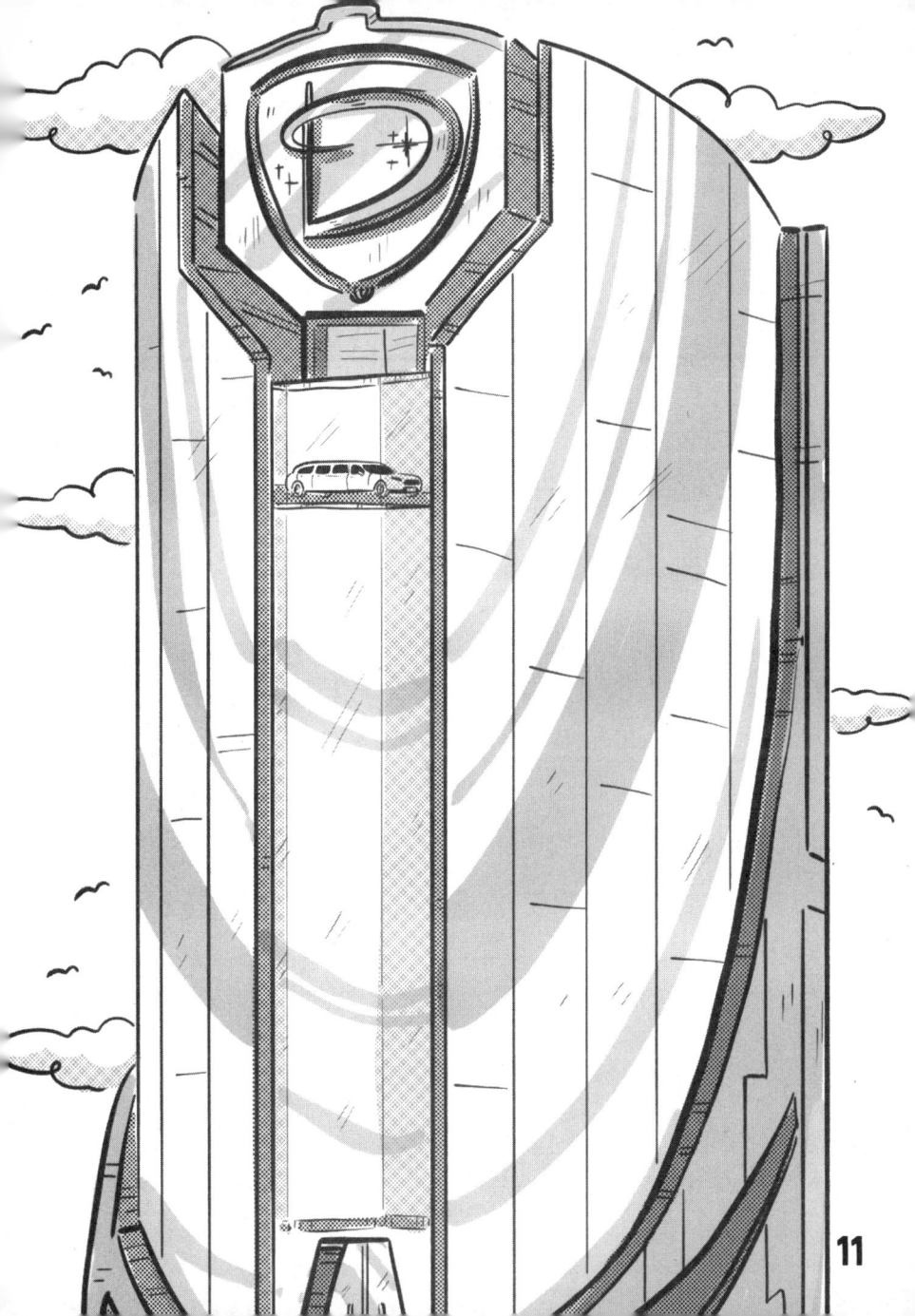

"Tech is so cool," I said.

And it was, until robot arms sprang from the walls, lifted me off the floor, and squeezed me like a tube of toothpaste.

"*Never mind,*" I wheezed. "Tech is BAD! Tech is VERY BAD!"

"INTRUDER! INTRUDER!" a voice boomed.

But Regina didn't look worried. She just said, "Oh, sorry, that's my computer. Put him down, Jeff."

The robot arms released me, and I wondered if this place had a robot gym. Because those robot arms were super strong.

Then a bigger question popped into my head.

"You named your computer *Jeff?*" I asked.

"Yep," said Regina. "It was either that or Barry. Could you imagine?"

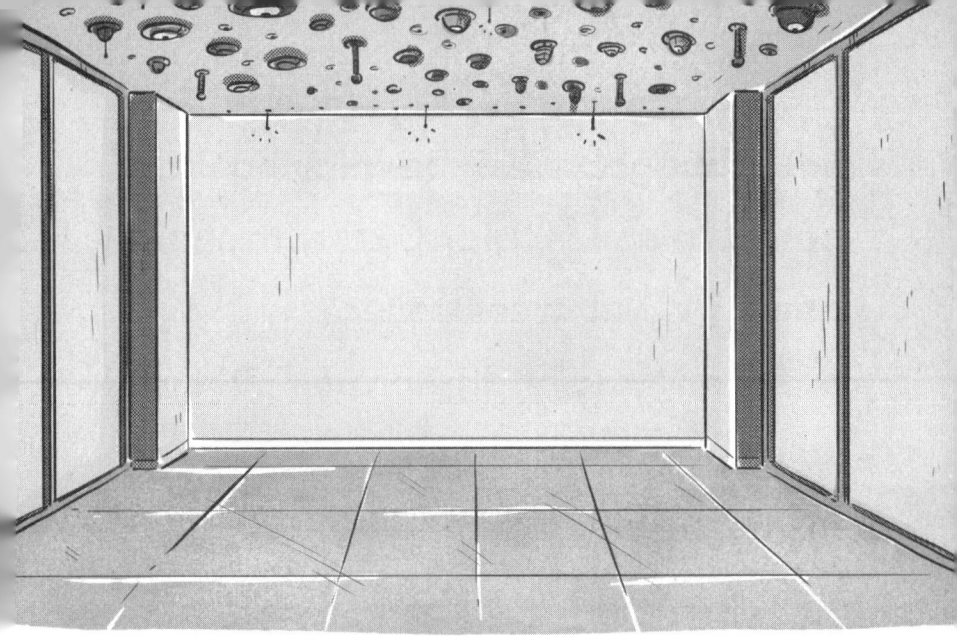

Hmm, I did not know what to say to that. But I was used to being speechless around Regina. I mean, we just rode up a limo elevator.

Behind the door was an empty room. The walls were white. The floor was white. And the ceiling was . . . you guessed it... *made of high-tech sensors.*

"I thought we'd be playing in a normal place," I said. "Like, with chairs and a TV with a controller."

"I don't really *do* normal," Regina said. "See, you are going to be playing *inside* the video game."

Wait. Was Regina going to beam me into the game? What if I got trapped inside? That would not be fun.

"Don't worry, I'm not going to trap you in the video game," she said as if she could read my mind. "But you will need this."

Jeff's robot arms returned holding some kind of space suit.

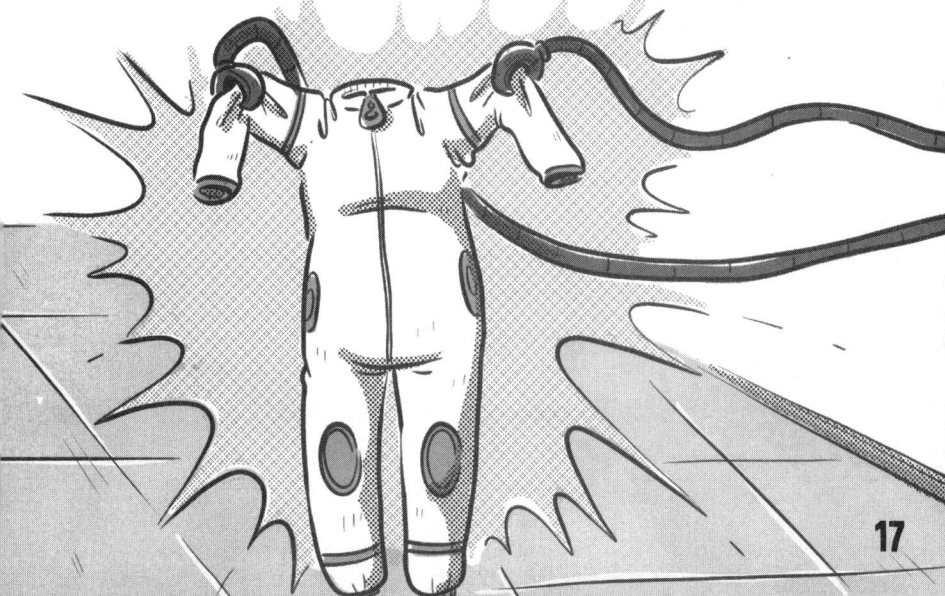

"The suit is your controller," said Regina. "Try it on."

Before I could say *please don't pick me up again,* Jeff picked me up again and smushed me into the space suit.

When he put me down, a character version of me appeared on the wall screen.

I lifted my arm. It did too. We even danced the same exact way!

"It's like looking in a mirror!" I said.

"Yeah, you've both got the wrong kind of funky moves," said Regina. "Now, while you control your character with the suit, I can use my controller to help when you need it. That's what sets my game apart. If you're bad, I can make you better."

"Sounds easy!" I said as I put on my special game helmet.

Spoiler alert: nothing in my world was ever easy.

But it could be fun!

CHEAT CODE UNLOCKED

The game started with, what else, *a floating start button.*

I reached out to tap it.

With a *CLICK*, stars erupted all around me and the ceiling turned into fluffy purple clouds. The floor became a green field of grass that sparkled.

I was no longer in the white room. I was inside a VIDEO GAME WORLD!

"Regina, you're a *Reg-genius!*" I said.

Just then, another voice spoke. It was the voice of the game. "Welcome, Player One . . . to PERFECT PIXEL PUPS!"

That's when a pack of digital doggies bounded toward me with tails wagging and collars jingling. Oh no, could they smell me?

"Ugh, why am I cursed with smelling like roast beef?" I yelled at the digital sky.

I cringed as the dogs leaped, then froze in midair.

Their tongues were so close I could see slobber droplets.

"What happened?" I asked.

"I used the PAWS button!" Regina joked.

I couldn't see Regina, but I could hear her tapping away and making things happen in the game world.

Tap! The pups were airlifted away.

Tap tap! A treasure chest appeared.

"Uh-oh, are pirates coming?" I asked.

"Lulz, no. We're gonna choose your avatar," Regina explained. "An avatar is your character in the game. Think of it like your outfit."

Regina had created thousands of awesome avatars. I reached into the treasure chest and transformed into a werewolf.

"Too itchy!" I said.

Then I picked out a punk-rock unicorn.

"Too sparkly!" I said.

"Just pick one," Regina begged. "I don't want to spend the whole day on which avatar you like."

"Then why did you make so many?" I asked.

Robot surfer.

Jet-pack llama.

Pineapple man.

I wanted to be them all!

"This is taking too long," said Regina. "I'm making you ... a wizard."

Tap! I was now a wizard with a long gray beard.

"Aww, not cool! I don't feel *wizardy*," I said. "Let me pick who I want to be."

I stumbled into the treasure chest and the whole digital world went black.

"Cheat code unlocked," the video game voice announced. "Welcome to VILLAIN MODE."

"Nope," said Regina.

Then she tapped another button and the suit forced me to move. But I didn't want to go anywhere.

"Stop!" I said, and tripped over my long wizard beard.

"Oh no! What did you do?" Regina asked.

"Oh no! What *did* I do?!" I asked too!

Suddenly I was surrounded by all the evil villain characters Regina had designed for the game. And they did not look happy to see me.

"Avatar selected!" said the video-game voice.

I looked down and my wizard outfit was gone. I was back to being my regular digital self.

Except now . . . I was a *mini* boss.

4

THE MINI BOSS GAME

So, what's a mini boss?

No, it's not a tiny elf that tells people what to do!

Mini bosses are low-level video-game villains you have to beat before the big boss battle. Some are easy, some are tough, and yes, some are even short.

No matter what they look like, they're all baddies with bad attitudes. And I was surrounded by a whole mob of them.

"Regina," I whispered. "You're restarting the game, right? To get me away from these goons? Right?"

"We can hear you too, you know," said a cyclops holding a flaming torch.

"Well, I know that now," I said.

"We can't restart," said Regina. "It would look like something was wrong with the game, and I could lose my *extra* extra credit."

Clearly, this *extra* extra credit was *extra* extra important to Regina. And I couldn't let her down. I'd lost track of how many times she'd helped me out, so I decided to do something for her.

I'd be *extra* extra brave.

"Hey," I said. "We can still get your credit. I'll just play as a mini boss!"

"Really?" said Regina. "Perfect! Just don't move while I find someone else to be the hero."

So I waited.

And waited.

But I guess mini bosses don't do much until they're called into action. They just sit in a back-room part of the video game most players never see.

But the good news was that the other mini bosses didn't seem to notice me.

The Gorilla Gladiators just played on their phones. The Spider Monsters tossed boomerangs at a bull's-eye. And the Walking Shark Man?

He was strutting up to me with a smile full of razor-sharp shark teeth.

"I ain't seen you around before," the shark man said. "You don't look scary at all. What's your power? Are you just too sweet?"

All the other mini bosses laughed.

"Nah, he's one of those weak mini bosses that players just jump over," said the cyclops.

"Or he could be a spy," said the shark with a look in his eyes I did not like at all.

It was the same way I looked at delicious candy, like I couldn't wait to take a big bite.

Okay, so much for being brave and waiting for Regina.

I bolted out of the crowd and ran for the side door labeled LEVEL ENTRANCE.

"Hey! You can't go there!" the shark man roared. "That door is for PLAYERS only!"

"Well, there's a first time for everything!" I shouted back as the door swung closed behind me.

5

NOT READY, PLAYER ONE!

I burst back into the welcome screen. Only I didn't feel very welcome this time.

The clouds looked worried. The Pixel Pups stayed back. Even the video game voice sounded confused.

"Welcome . . . *mini boss?*" the voice said. "No, no. This does not compute."

"It's cool. I'm Player One," I told everyone. "I'm just waiting for Regina to get back."

But the pups weren't having it.

"This is the *woofiest worst-est*," one pup said.

"A mini boss?" scoffed another pup. "You've gone to the *bark* side."

They looked at me like I was their enemy. I may have been in a colorful video-game world, but now I felt like I was *in the doghouse*.

"Guys, I'm still me," I tried to explain. "The same kid who smells like roast beef!"

"No," the biggest pup said. "You *ARF* not welcome here. You must go *bark-bark-BACK* to the mini-boss room."

The other pups agreed and opened the side door I'd just come through!

"Wait! Don't!" I screamed.

But it was too late. The door swung open and a stampede of mini bosses came rushing through.

And they weren't looking for me. They were looking for the treasure chest, which was filled with power-ups and special skills these mini bosses had never seen.

"Looky here," snickered the shark man. "We mini bosses are gonna be UNSTOPPABLE!"

The pups and I looked at one another.

"*Ruh-oh,*" the tiniest pup said. "Run!"

Trust me on this one: when cute little puppies tell you to run, you better run.

I moved my legs as fast as I could, but even in the game, I still ran like the real me: slow and clumsy. It wasn't pretty.

I trip over my own sneakers all the time. Now I was going to have to *speed run* every level!

That's when the video-game voice gave me a warning that I already knew.

"You are NOT ready, Player One!"

6

THE GAME STRIKES BACK!

The game world changed to sky-blue pixels. My feet were on puffs of white high above everything else.

What was I standing on? It definitely wasn't the ground.

So that's when I looked down. Everything below me was teeny-tiny like it was far, far away.

And yep, the kid who gets scared just *hearing* the phrase "roller coaster" was now standing where airplanes soar.

I was in Cloud Town. The buildings and roads were made of clouds. So were the people, who were Level One enemies. They formed out of thin air.

If I weren't so totally freaked out, I would have totally geeked out over Regina's game design. It was a work of art. Very real . . . maybe too real. I did not want to fall to my doom.

Then I remembered the real me was safe in the skyscraper, sliding around Regina's office with a weird suit on. And sure, I probably looked really silly. But that's never stopped me before.

So I gulped and grabbed a cloud zipline that sent me flying over Cloud Town. It still gave me that *barf-ish* feeling in my stomach.

Especially since the mini bosses had bounced their way up here.

And boy, were they messing up the level! The mini bosses were destroying Cloud Town, making everything go *POOF*!

And since I didn't want to go POOF, I kept going.

That's when I bumped on a big, floating arrow pointing to a Cloud House. The game clearly wanted me to go here to complete the level. I rode the cloud through the front window.

There were no enemies inside. Just some cloud furniture and a mysterious back door that was locked.

A locked door usually needed a special key in video games. And that key was always in the hands of a mini boss you had to battle.

"Wait a sec," I realized. *"I'm* a mini boss!"

I reached into my pocket and pulled out a glowing golden key! I'd had it the whole time because I was the mini boss of Cloud Town!

Wait. Did that also mean I was the *weakest* mini boss in the game?

Not cool.

But also not cool: the real dangerous mini bosses heading my way. I could hear their evil laughs echo through the game.

"Mini boss, come out to playyy-ayyyy!" they called to me.

But I wasn't going to play their game. I had the key to Level Two.

All I had to do was open the door and walk through to the other side.

And I was not the only fish in the sea.

I held my breath as shadows circled me. Maybe they would be nice little seahorses or adorable baby shrimp?

Nah, they were giant piranhas with vampire fangs. Why did Regina have such a good imagination?!

One piranha swam up to me.

7

DON'T HOLD YOUR BREATH

There is one big problem with doors in video games: you never know what's on the other side.

This door opened to a steep drop.

I fell through the air and bounced off every cloud on the way down until... SPLASH!

Yep, Level Two was underwater.

"Are you holding your breath?" he asked.

"Um, yeah, I'm holding my breath," I said. "I'm underwater."

That made them all laugh, and there is nothing like getting laughed at by vampire piranhas.

"What's so funny?" I asked them.

"You don't need to hold your breath in a video game!" the piranha reminded me. "You're not even holding your breath now. You're talking."

Hmm, he had a point there.

I gulped and waited for the piranhas to attack, but they didn't.

"How do I play this level?" I asked. "Do I dodge you guys

all the way until I reach the end?"

This made them laugh again. I guess I'm really funny to piranhas?

"You're a mini boss," said a piranha. "Just wait here with us and attack the player once they swim into the level."

"Oh, right!" I said. "I *am* a mini boss! That means I'm on the bad-guy side."

"Well, we're not really *bad* guys," said the piranha. "We're just coded that way. The game might not be fun if we weren't here."

Hmm, these piranhas were super smart. Because they just gave me the best idea. I could beat all the levels just by being a mini boss!

While the piranhas waited for the next player to drop from the sky, I snuck away.

I swam past even more underwater monsters and enemies. The game had an octopus with fireball tentacles, tons of flying fishhooks, and a squad of snapping clams!

They all let me pass unharmed because they knew a mini boss when they saw one coming.

Was my plan going to work?

Um, no. Because the next players to drop in were the *REAL* mini bosses.

"STOP THAT MINI BOSS!" commanded the shark man. "HE'S A FAKE!"

PLAYER TWO GOES BOOM!

I had never fake swum so fast in my life.

In the real world, I could feel my arms flapping and flapping through the air.

In the video game world, I WAS BEING CHASED BY ALL THE BAD GUYS!

But I had something they did not: a head start.

I reached the door to Level Three and burst through like it was the end of a race!

"*LEVEL THREE!*" the voice of the game announced as I suddenly swam up onto a golden shore.

Ahhh, dry land. No more soggy avatar.

I shook off the water pixels and saw a castle in the distance. I was in a fairy-tale land. There were townsfolk making pies, jugglers juggling pies, and an army of knights eating pies.

Oh, and everyone was watching me.

"Invader!" the knights called out.

"To the dungeons with him!" one knight commanded.

Hmm, maybe I should have been the wizard avatar Regina wanted me to be. I would be magic . . . and magic beats knights all the time.

Instead, I'd have to trick these guys the old-fashioned way—by making something up.

"Wait!" I said. "I am, uh ... your new mini boss!"

They stopped in their tracks.

"If you're the new mini boss, then what is the king's name?" asked a knight.

"Uhhh . . . King *Barry*?" I guessed.

"Barry?! That's a *Barry silly* name," the knight said. "Everyone knows the real king's name is Jeff."

"*Really? Another Jeff?!*" I exclaimed.

They drew their swords on me again.

"Hail, King Jeff!" the knights chanted. "Capture the *Barry sneaky imposter!*"

Okay, time to run. I darted through the crowd and hoofed it to the castle. I could hear the knights in armor clanking behind me!

"Some help would be great right now," I screamed. "Regina? ANYONE? HELP!"

That's when I heard a booming voice announce, "Enter . . . PLAYER TWO!"

A bolt of lightning struck the ground beside me and when the dust cleared, there was a giant towering over me.

The new player stood as tall as the castle. I couldn't tell if she was friendly or not, but I felt like I'd seen her somewhere before.

"Glinda?" I asked.

Of course, Glinda Alegre, the shortest kid in my grade, would play as the biggest character ever!

"That's right, *little* guy," laughed the Giant Glinda. "Regina said you needed help?"

"And I'm here too!" a voice said back in the real world. It sounded like confidence and perfect hair. It was my best buddy, Jake Gold.

"Jake!" I cheered.

"I'm standing next to you in this white room and giving you a bear hug," Jake said. "You probably can't tell."

I could. My avatar looked like it was levitating off the ground and being squeezed by an invisible hugger.

I didn't care. I was just happy to be with my friends again!

But there was no time to celebrate. The knights were charging toward us. And they'd brought some help, too.

The shark man and the other mini bosses came ready for battle.

"You guys any good at video games?" I asked.

"I like making things go BOOM," Giant Glinda said. "Does that count?"

"And I can mash buttons *really hard*," Jake said.

"Okay then," I said as the army of enemies surrounded us. "GAME ON!"

9

AS EASY AS PIE

The epic battle was about to begin and I was nervous.

I had never made it this far in a video game. I had no clue what to do.

But I wasn't alone. I had Giant Glinda and Invisible Jake on my side.

If you think three kids against an army sounds impossible, don't worry.

It gets, like ... way worse. you know, as things usually do for me.

Because the bad guys had a catapult now. They wheeled it out onto the battlefield, along with every pie in the kingdom. They were going to launch them at us like delicious cannonballs!

"Your defeat will be SWEET!" the shark man cackled.

"Is it too late to hit the reset button?" I whispered.

But then a little voice in the back of my head said, "Don't give up. You can do this."

Okay, so it wasn't a little voice inside my head. It was Regina's voice talking to me through the game helmet!

"You're at the final level!" said Regina. "Let me take control and we can finish this together."

"Aww yeah!" I cheered. "You mini bosses are in trouble now!"

I felt Regina take control and move my suit into an awesome pose, like when a cool game character is about to unleash their special move. Whatever I was about to do was going to scare these mini bosses silly, I just knew it.

But instead of doing a spinning freeze-ray kick, or farting a furious fart-nado, my avatar just walked over and joined the mini bosses.

"Huh?" I asked. "What's going on, Regina?"

"You're a mini boss, remember?" she said. "I need you to lose so the real players can win the game. It's the only way to get the *extra* extra credit."

"Oh," I said.

As much as I didn't want to admit it, it made sense. But it didn't feel great.

I thought I was helping this whole time. Instead, I was a villain. And villains aren't supposed to win games. They are supposed to lose. And thanks to my rotten luck of making myself a villain, I was doomed to watch my friends get all the glory without me.

And that was not fun. Not fun at all.

I'd found yet another new way to embarrass myself in video games.

And that's when it hit me!

"Got a lightbulb?" I asked a knight.

"Sir, this is a medieval village," the knight explained. "Electricity has not been invented yet."

"That's too bad, because I just got a BRIGHT idea!" I said. "I know how to help my friends win! By doing what I do best...BEING THE WORST!"

First I took control over launching the pie catapult. Why? Because my aim was awful!

How awful? Every pie I flung managed to fly clear over the castle or accidentally hit one of the knights! I knocked a cyclops over with two tons of blueberry pie. He was mad and messy.

With a burst of banana cream pie, I bowled over some Gorilla Gladiators. Then, I knocked down some Spider Monsters in a web of whipped cream!

I wasted *thousands* of pies, and not a single bit of crust got near Giant Glinda's face.

"Your aim stinks!" Glinda told me. "Nice job!"

"The sad part is I am actually *trying* to hit you!" I explained with a laugh.

Glinda raced toward the castle, where I could see four familiar furry blocks. It was the Pixel Pups! They were gathered on the castle roof and waving a glowing golden flag.

This was our chance to claim victory!

The shark man was furious. He ran to stop Glinda but slipped in some pie goop and fell flat on his back . . . fin first!

"ACK!" the shark man cried. "Our battle is ruined! You are the worst mini boss I've ever met!"

"You bet I am," I said as Giant Glinda headed toward the castle.

She grabbed the flag from the pups and waved it high in the air!

The pups howled with excitement and jumped for joy!

The mini bosses were all defeated and covered in pie.

Well, every mini boss except me.

Then the announcer said the five sweetest words I'd heard all day:

"HIP-PUP-HOORAY! PLAYERS WIN!"

10

GAME OVER

Fireworks exploded above the castle. Confetti rained down. Then trumpets played and people cheered. We had done it. We'd finished *Perfect Pixel Pups*.

There were a lot of good things about the game being over. First, Regina earned her *extra* extra credit.

The second was I had actually helped my friend.

But the third and maybe best thing was I could finally leave the digital world and go back to being my regular self in the real world.

A wonderful feeling came over me. Followed by a very tight squeeze.

"Jake, are you giving me another gold-medal hug?" I asked.

"Um, that's so not me, dude," said Jake.

I took off my helmet and entered the real world, where Robo-Octo had wrapped around me.

"Cool octopus," said Glinda. "I like the way he crushes you."

"Thanks?" I gasped.

Then Regina ran over.

"Robo-Octo, off!" she said, and the octopus let go. "Now it's my turn for a hug!"

And I swear Regina's hug might have been the strongest of all.

Then Jake picked us all up with a monster bear hug. Even Robo-Octo could not escape his giant arms.

"Congrats, bro!" Jake cheered. "You beat the game with your magic power of being awkward at everything!"

"I feel pretty awkward right now," I said. "Maybe you could put us down?"

"Oh, right," said Jake as he set us back on the ground.

Then, the real-world Glinda made an announcement.

"Your pie-flinging made those poor innocent townsfolk fear for their lives," she said with an evil smile. "I like your bad-guy style. We make a pretty good team."

"I guess we do," I agreed.

Then Regina pulled me aside.

"Thanks for your help. And I'm sorry," she said. "I should have trusted you to finish the game on your own instead of taking control."

"Eh, you were only trying to help," I said. "And so was I."

"Same here!" Glinda said.

"Me too!" Jake added.

Even Robo-Octo raised his tentacle.

Looking around at my friends and a robot octopus, I realized something.

Whether you're the worst player in every level like me.

Or a giant show-off who knows all the BIG special moves like Glinda.

Or you just like to watch others play from the background, staying invisible like Jake.

When it comes to video games, everyone *belongs*. Every Player One will always need a Player Two.

Or Three. Maybe even a group of four!

Or EIGHT . . . if you're an octopus.

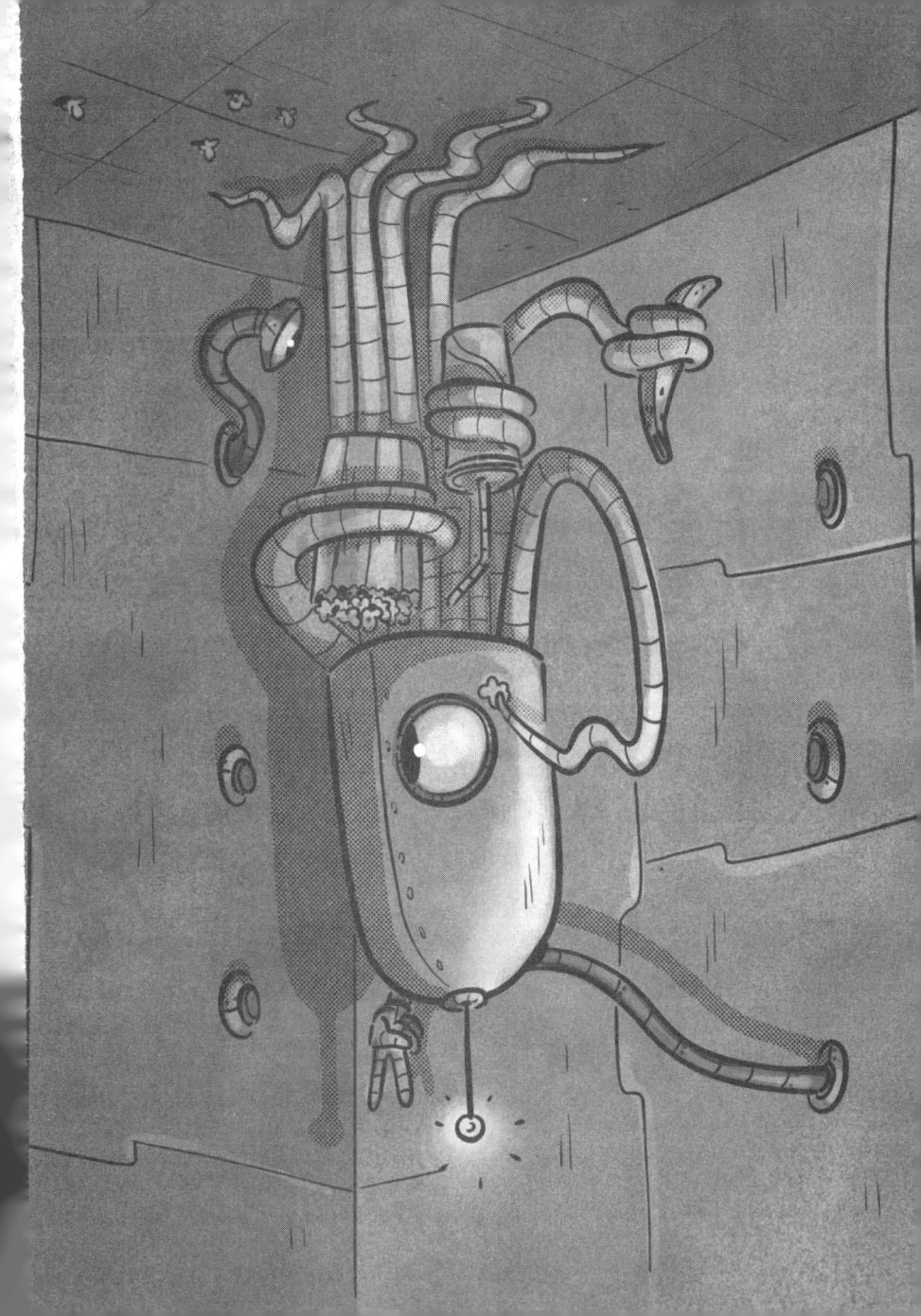

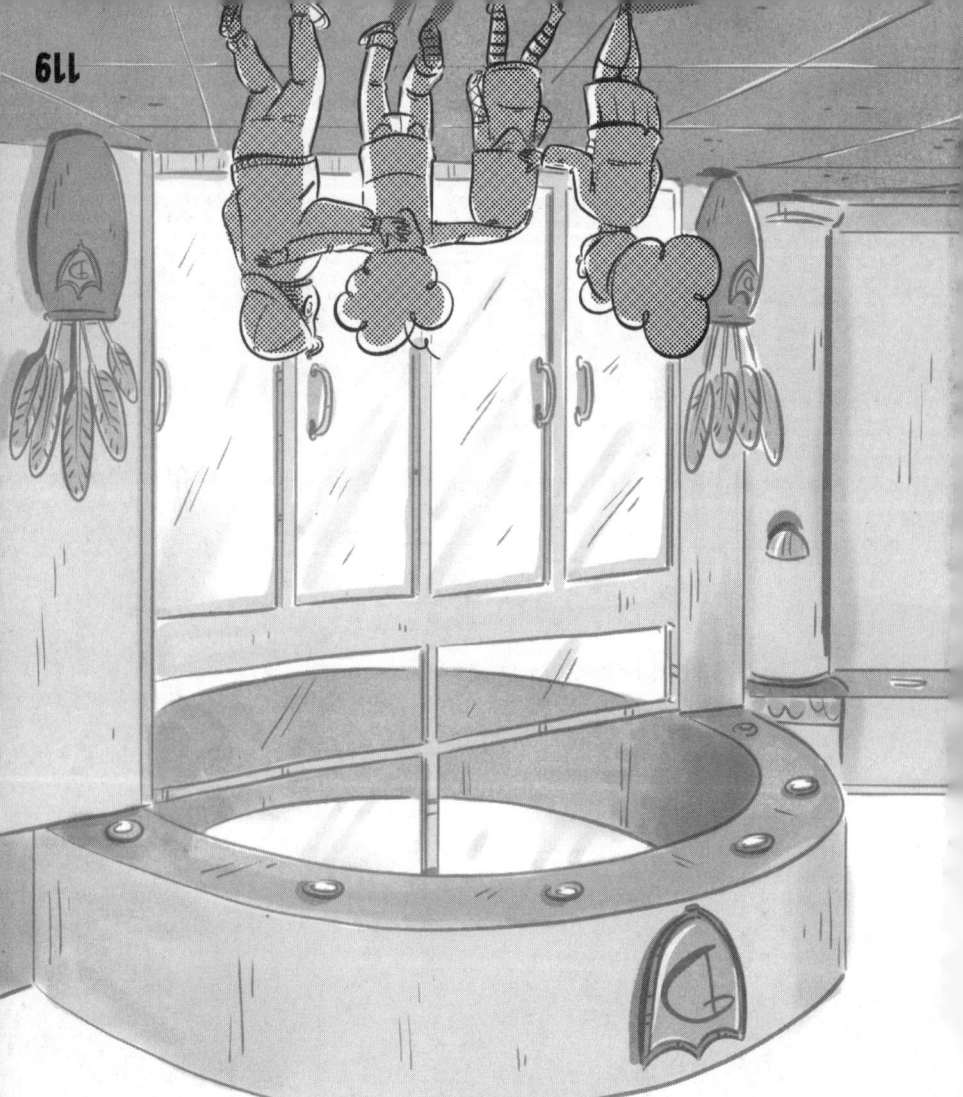

Or Three. Maybe even a group of four! Or EIGHT... if you're an octopus.